I0717797

The Rolodex Happenings
Dennis James Sweeney

STILL
HOUSE
PRESS

All inquiries may be directed to:

Stillhouse Press
4400 University Drive, 3E4
Fairfax, VA 22030
www.stillhousepress.org

Excerpts from this work originally appeared in *New Delta Review, Sleepingfish, and Tammy*

Stillhouse Press is an independent, student- and alumni-run nonprofit press based out of Northern Virginia and operated in collaboration with Watershed Lit: Center for Literary Engagement and Publishing Practice at George Mason University.

Library of Congress Control Number: 2023947279

ISBN-13: 978-1-945233-25-8

Jacket Design and Back Image: Christopher Kardambikis
Cover and Interior Photo Images Courtesy of the Sweeney Family
Interior Design: Paul Logan IV

Permissions

Where Have All The Flowers Gone?
Words and Music by Pete Seeger
Copyright © 1955 Sanga Music Inc.
Copyright Renewed
All Rights Administered by Figs. D Music
c/o Concord Music Publishing
All Rights Reserved   Used by Permission
Reprinted by Permission of Hal Leonard LLC

Thank you to University of California Press for permission to quote from Allan Kaprow's *Essays on the Blurring of Art and Life.* Pages 22, 7-9, and 219.

*These are our greenest days. Some of us will become famous,
and we will have proven once again that the only success
occurred when there was a lack of it.*

—Allan Kaprow, "'Happenings' in the New York Scene"

Table of Contents

Introduction

Two Augusts ago, my father died, and my mother asked me to go through his possessions, keep what I wanted, give a few key items to my brother, and dispense with everything else. My father was given to bouts of nostalgia. Ever since I can remember, he would retreat to our garage on Sunday afternoons to sort through the refuse of a life lived: an old SCUBA mask, a wrinkled felt flag, a clarinet case without a clarinet. He was not a recluse, not even an eccentric, but it was understood in our family that his moments in the garage were not to be interrupted. As children, Bob and I would wait in the yard for him to emerge and hoist us in the air again, asking one of his famous questions: If you were a bird, which tree would you live in? If you were a flower, when would you bloom?

I did most of my archeological work stripped to the waist in St. Louis's oppressive heat. By that time I hadn't used a sick day for years, so I was able to take off an entire month to sort through my father's things. Which was more time than I needed, but this was my father, and even then I understood you can't treat the grieving process with kid gloves. As for Bob, he was still struggling to piece together an acting career in New York, and I supported him in that. I called and left a message saying I'd send what I thought would be of interest to him to the most recent address he had given me.

On my third day in St. Louis, as I sat beside a trash can, a "Keep" box, and a rapidly expanding "Maybe" pile, my mother wandered into the garage for the first time since I'd been home. She picked up a few objects and examined them, then remarked abruptly that my father had kept a Rolodex and she thought I ought to have it.

"A Rolodex?"

She nodded.

"Of addresses?"

"I don't know," she said. "Maybe." She walked to a cluttered sawhorse table and picked up a heap of yellowing cards that curled above a rusting gray stand. She had known exactly where it was. After handing it to me, she said she was making grilled cheese for both of us and returned promptly to the house.

The Rolodex's sudden appearance intrigued me. In the mass of my father's useless, inexplicable doodads—a splintered baseball bat, a half-unraveled straw hat, a mason jar of sand—here was an object I wouldn't have to speculate about but could simply *read*. I flipped through the typewritten cards and found that they contained not addresses but events, labeled by date and described in wide-eyed detail. The cards were marked with stains and typographical errors, crossed out by hand or typewritten *x*'s, and frayed soft at the edges as if they had been touched repeatedly. Besides these imperfections the cards were remarkably plain, without alphabetical markers or color-coded organizational tabs. They were simply old sheets of cardstock with text pressed into them, bound to their center by two thin metal rings. At the end, photographs were crammed into the Rolodex: my father, my brother, me.

Once I began to read the entries in earnest, I discovered that the Rolodex was filled with Happenings, the artistic kind pioneered by Allan Kaprow, and that they described not only moments of play and odd joy but instances of sexual awakening, jealousy, and personal fear. I knew very little about Happenings then. The name Allan Kaprow meant nothing to me. I gleaned only that my father had engaged in the kind of transgressive performance art I associated with the 1960s, and that he had used the Rolodex to record each event.

I read until I knew I would be missed in the kitchen. When I went inside, my mother was standing over the counter slicing two grilled cheese sandwiches into sailboats, the way she had when Bob and I were boys. I sat at the table and watched her slide the sandwiches onto plates, adding a dollop of potato salad to each. She placed mine in front of me and sat. For a while we chewed.

Finally I asked my mother about the Happenings. She looked at me suspiciously, as if she were on the verge of denying their existence altogether. I sensed she had hoped I wouldn't ask, saving her from explaining my own father to me. Then she sighed, pushed away her plate, and folded her hands in her lap.

"I think of it as a stage, honey."

"A stage?"

"We all go through stages." She sipped her water. "Like your brother."

I raised my eyebrows. Bob had been in New York for sixteen years.

"Before we came to Missouri, your father ran with a loose crowd. Timothy, for example. Still unemployed.

We send him a Christmas card every year. He's never sent one back."[*]

"Mom—"

"He was handsome, sure. But that only gets you so far."

"Mom."

"They lived in that terrible house on Celso Street for eight years. But your father had to pull his life together." She nodded toward me. "We came to St. Louis so we could have you."

"But you were in California that whole time too," I said.

"I was." She stared at the single sailboat remaining on her plate. Then she looked out the kitchen window in the direction of the garage.

"Why'd you give it to me?" I asked.

She sighed grandly, as if we had already finished the conversation. She crossed her arms and said: "I just didn't want it anymore."

She pulled her plate toward her and raised the remaining sailboat to her lips, even though it was cold

---

[*] Later, when I began to press my mother for answers, I learned that "Timothy" is the man my father refers to in the Rolodex as Shackleton.

by now, the cheese congealed at its edges. I watched her eat in silence. When she was finished, I cleared the dishes and loaded them in the washer.

Then I went back to the garage.

My father's Rolodex entries consist of a series of performances that took place between 1960 and 1972. They are grouped most thickly during the early '60s and thin out toward the end of the decade, when my parents' courtship began to "get serious," as my mother puts it. Many of them consist of planned enactments, recorded with a casual air that seems kindred with Allan Kaprow's own scrappy maintenance of the materials behind his Happenings. Other entries, however, include accounts of events that might only in retrospect be considered Happenings, set down in writing out of the simple impulse to record.

Many entries couldn't fit on a single Rolodex card. These were typed front and back and carried over to the next card in the stack. Although there were 47 Happenings in my father's file, they filled a total of 119 Rolodex cards. The longest note, detailing my father and Shackleton's effort to sabotage a friend's physical exam after he was drafted for Vietnam, comprises the front and back of eight separate cards.

The twelve photographs tucked at the end of the Rolodex seem to be both an extension of the Happenings and a refutation of them. Like the Happenings, they are not in strict chronological order. Unlike the Happenings, they go uncommented upon. It is as if my father wished to continue constructing the Rolodex but at a certain point found that he had run out of words.

That point, I have found, is where my words begin. I have therefore added my own captions to the photographs.

During the very years that my father's involvement in his Happenings declined, Allan Kaprow himself moved to the West Coast and, in 1974, began his tenure at the University of California, San Diego. I am certain that my father never met Kaprow, and almost as certain that he never knew how near Kaprow had come to Celso Street. By the time I was old enough to create memories, my father had concentrated his artistic pursuits, as far as I can tell, in computer-aided technologies for newspaper design. During my childhood, my father certainly gave the appearance of having been born to be a father. As I grew up and moved away, the slow rhythms of his life began to seem unbearable. My chief goal was not to become him.

What I did not realize was that he had once been as young as I was. Younger even, judging by the free-wheeling spirit of his Happenings. His choices were not so different from my brother's—choices I never realized I could make.

In an essay introducing a critical volume on the subject, Michael Kirby emphasizes the Happenings' intentionality. His working definition: "a *purposefully composed form of theatre in which diverse alogical elements, including nonmatrixed performing, are organized in a compartmented structure.*"[*] My father's implicit definition of a Happening was as far removed from this as San Diego is from New York. He and Shackleton took the "alogical" component of the Happenings to the contextual, identifying nearly any out-of-the-ordinary behavior as a Happening, regardless of whether it was—in fact, especially when it was *not*—subject to a planned context or even structure. Particularly with regard to audience, the Rolodex Happenings preferred to surprise

---

[*]   Michael Kirby, "Happenings: An Introduction," *Happenings and Other Acts*, 11. Kirby's italics. What Kirby means by "nonmatrixed," I think, is that the question of whether or not each part of the performance is meant to be a performance is not resolved by the substance of the performance itself.

and infiltrate, rather than to invite and transfix as the East Coast artists tended to do.[*]

But they wouldn't have formulated it that way. Instead, I think my father's circle was simply "playing" under the convenient aegis of an artistic movement Shackleton encountered during a visit to New Jersey. This allowed them both to retain their legitimacy as artists and to act like impudent children. What more could an unemployed, uninspired painter in his twenties ask for?

From the beginning, the Happenings insulated them from the realities of their era. Their Pet Liberation Army,

---

[*] That said, the two camps' ideals, if not their actual performances, were sympathetic. In his seminal essay "The Legacy of Jackson Pollock," Kaprow writes: "Not only will these bold creators show us, as if for the first time, the world we have always had about us but ignored, but they will disclose entirely unheard-of happenings and events, found in garbage cans, police files, hotel lobbies; seen in store windows and on the streets; and sensed in dreams and horrible accidents. An odor of crushed strawberries, a letter from a friend, or a billboard selling Drano; three taps on the front door, a scratch, a sigh, or a voice lecturing endlessly, a blinding staccato flash, a bowler hat—all will become materials for this new concrete art." Allan Kaprow, "The Legacy of Jackson Pollock (1958)," *Essays on the Blurring of Art and Life*, 7-9.

for example, was almost certainly in conversation with the global rise of communism and America's brutal opposition to it. But which side did my father take? He and his friends acted disruptively but not politically, as if the stakes of their actions were no more than personal. Perhaps this was the exact thrill of the Happenings: the feeling that, because they had no argument, they could get away with anything.

As Allan Kaprow wrote with regard to the six parts of the historical first Happening at Reuben Gallery in Manhattan on October 4, 1959: "Each of these parts may be re-arranged indefinitely."[*] The entries here, when I came upon them, were ordered as they appear below—likely due to my father's late-life riffling, which my mother tells me he engaged in until his very last days. Instead of restoring their chronology, I have chosen to present both the Happenings and the photographs in the order in which I found them. The present arrangement seems fitting to me, as if the Happenings have always been younger than either of us, pulling us back to a place I never knew I needed to go.

If you need to, cut them out and rearrange them.

____

[*]   *Allan Kaprow: 18/6: 18 Happenings in 6 Parts, 9/10/11 November 2006*, 45.

If you would like to, re-enact them or revise them.
Regardless, recall: They were once alive. In my opinion,
they still are.

> *—Guy Sutter, Jr.*
> *Los Angeles*

The Rolodex Happenings

[1960 March]

So we tried it out. We stood on the sidewalk handing pieces of paper to the shoppers, me on one side of the street and Shackleton on the other. Willie joined us last minute and decided to stand in the middle of the road, holding out slivers of paper to the cars. A couple people slowed down and actually took them. The thing was the papers were blank. They said nothing on them. Most of the shoppers thought we were advertising people, the kind who hand out quarter-sheets for a vacuum sale. Then a few steps down the sidewalk they would look at the paper. You'd see their walk slow and they'd flip the paper over. Some of them turned around and looked at me. I waved and smiled with all my teeth. The idea was that I, as opposed to the vacuum cleaner salesmen, believed in what I was selling. Which was the void. You know, emptiness. The freedom to expand.

[1960 May]

We dressed up in workout clothes—Shackleton wore an elastic sweatband—and we went to the gymnasium. We brought a balloon with us. Turned out you had to be a member to get in but we told them we wanted to try it out before we joined, and I guess because there were four of us it seemed like a business opportunity so they let us in. Even with the balloon. The gym smelled like chalk and sweat. There were guys bigger than everything I've ever eaten loading bars heavier than themselves onto their necks. Veins. Red skin. A conspicuous absence of music. We walked to the middle of the weight room—me, Shackleton, Kerry, and Tab—they were the only two women in the place—and started playing keep-the-balloon-up-in-the-air. The meatheads got angry when they saw what we were doing. It was a real workout for us, and by the end we were sweating hard.

But you could see by the way they looked at us that we were not welcome there. We kept playing anyway. After a while a big man with the kind of shirt that was meant only to cover his nipples came over and batted at the balloon a couple times. Of course Tab thought he wanted to play and she flicked it in his direction. He grabbed it out of the air and pressed it between his hands until it burst. His palms turned white. We figured out later that they already had been white, from chalk, but the man was eerie and huge and our eyes followed him as he walked away. We had agreed that the balloon popping would be the end of the Happening, so we shrugged and pulled up our socks. The whole place swelled with blood.

[1960 November]

Kerry's dad owned a scuba shop and had some extra equipment on hand, so we donned it and went to the mall where they had a fountain you throw pennies into. It was hard to walk with the flippers but that was part of the point. We stopped in front of the fountain and started to discuss how we were going to recover the pennies: they were only two feet beneath the surface of the water but the ripples occluded their exact position and the pennies were likely slippery on the tile and we had scuba gloves on, which made our pinching capabilities unwieldy. We stood there for approximately an hour deliberating. Kerry held an empty plastic bucket in her hand. She kept glancing into it sadly, then back at the fountain. We obstructed the walkway a little, which a security guard came by and informed us of. We liked this. It forced us to move closer to the water, which the idea was we were actually afraid of, although we were dressed in scuba outfits and couldn't by any rights be scared of a two-foot pool. During the deliberations some of us put our faces so near the water our noses almost broke the surface tension, then pulled away in fright. Shoppers noticed. They gave us a wide berth. In the end we decided against trying for the pennies, although the preparations had taken such a long time. The secret was that the preparations—the deliberations—the standing around cringing at the water in scuba suits—were the Happening. Kerry's dad had wanted us to carry a sign or at least tack something to the back of our suits to advertise his scuba shop and we had said we would, but we left the sign in the truck. It would have ruined the effect. We clopped out of the mall hitching our oxygen up on our backs. We changed into jeans in the parking lot. Mr. Polk was proud later because he didn't know we had left his sign where we did. He puffed up his chest, patted the oxygen tanks, and told us they were full.

[1960 November]

We went to the Fine Arts Gallery and did the same with a painting of the ocean. It was a little harder to get inside but in the end there was no specific ban on scuba equipment, so they just had the security guards follow us around. They pulled closer when we stopped in front of a painting by Eugène Boudin. One ship was getting ready to leave the rocky shore, and two ships had already left. This time we debated whether it was too late to catch the ships that were on their way out to sea. On the one hand we were fast enough swimmers. Kerry, who had grown up in the ocean, might be able to catch the near one. On the other hand both ships were receding into the distance even as we spoke and would only grow farther away as we swam. This seemed to us a tragedy. Particularly because it was all academic. The ships were frozen in time—had been since 1890—and anyway the painting was made of paint and couldn't be entered by living people like us. You could have argued either way. That the moment was gone forever, or that the moment was forever preserved. In the end we had to leave. Mr. Polk needed his scuba suits back by sundown, and Tab was shifting from side to side like she wanted to smoke. So we left, clopping in our flippers to the exit. One of the guards accidentally accompanied us out the door. We shared cigarettes on the steps out front and Tab asked him if he would like one. A blank washed over his eyes when he realized he had left the museum. He almost said yes, I think.

[1960 June]

Shackleton had that sweatband and he really wanted to make the most of it so we dressed up in workout clothes again and went to a restaurant called Le Carniet, which doesn't mean anything in French. We were not what you would call properly dressed for a night out at a French restaurant, even one with a fake French name, but we asked if we could be seated. The plan was we would thank the host and walk away when he said no, but he said yes. Yes, you can be seated. We looked at each other. Shackleton tugged at his tank top. There was a second when I thought we might go ahead and have a French meal even though the Happening was for all intents and purposes kaput. Then we remembered our empty wallets and bowed to the host as if he was our king and we his jesters, parsing the kingdom in jokes. We left Le Carniet at a slow lope. The host had worn a waxed mustache. His forehead glared with light. The problem, we figured once we slowed to a walk, was you couldn't tell who had been putting on who.

[1961 September]

The nap-in was a success. Although the house is small I would estimate thirty-five people were in attendance and what we discovered is that if you're tired enough you can sleep anywhere including on a hardwood floor. Nell wrapped her legs around me— she wanted to take it to the next level—which normally I wouldn't argue with—but as a chaperone I felt it was my duty to pursue the type of authentic sleep we were advocating for on this one. Eventually she gave in. The arguments of a dark room on a sunny day are multifold. We swam in dreams for an hour, let the long waves wash over us, talked to the gods of fear and imagination, spoke to a giant squirrel. But the waking was the best part. Waking always is. People began to get up and use the toilet, run a glass of water for themselves in the kitchen. The entire house creaked to life with the steps of people rubbing sleep out of their eyes. The pizza parlor was shocked. We ordered 18 pies, unspecified except that every one had to be a different type. We passed around the jar but no one paid. We were sour about it for a minute, then Willie's swollen face lit up and he pulled a blank check out of his wallet. It never came back so it must have been good. But the pizza: there was no question about good. The day is always more silent after a nap. And more so when all the mouths are chewing. You could almost hear the ocean as we ate, even though it's a mile away. I am certain there was a seagull right outside, possibly in the yard.

[1966 August]

Norma and I went down to the shore and watched the sun sink in the sea.[*] It was a good night. The sand stuck to our asses.

---

[*] Norma, I should clarify, is my mother.

[1963 November]

Kerry connected us with a man who was moving art galleries so Shackleton and I spent all day lugging paintings wrapped in butcher paper in and out of the back of Kerry's pickup. When it was finally lunch we were tired of everything being invisible so we took a big painting from the truck—it was longer than both of Shackleton's arms when he held them straight out— and wrestled it into Johnny's Delicatessen. We set it up against the wall across from the meat case and tore the paper off. It turned out to be a painting of a naked woman riding a pair of cows. Johnny's kid who runs the deli—Joey—a real people person—looked at the painting and from nowhere started to laugh. It wasn't something we had planned for but most people in the deli turned and looked because everyone wants to get in on a joke. The cows' legs were at all angles and the woman stood with a foot on either of them, mouth open like she was moaning. Joey was still laughing. I call that my meat lovers! he said. And pulled a couple of slabs of cold cuts out to slice. In the end the sandwiches were delicious. The kind of sandwich you want to bring home with you, light some candles, treat right. We left the painting there during lunch and loaded it back into the truck after we ate. Our fingers were greasy, but the smears suited it. The consensus was that the gallery guy didn't notice. He was too worried about his tie.

[1963 July]

Solo act. Back in Hartford. Mom and Dad were about to sell the old house so I went to see it one last time and help them pack boxes. When they were out, I crawled under the deck and scratched THIS IS MY HOUSE on the underside of one of the boards with a pocketknife. I couldn't tell which board it was when I got back on top of the deck so I crawled under again and stuck a stick through the gap between that board and the next one. When I climbed out and identified the board I had written on I peed on it, but my urine splashed across multiple planks. I can hardly stand the symbol. All I know is that when I was a child our cat crawled under there when it was her time to die. My dad had to pull her out with a rake because he didn't want to get on his hands and knees where she had just given up the ghost. We didn't bury her but took her to the vet to be taken care of. By the time my parents got home—the night of the Happening, I mean—they had been at a movie and had invited me to go but I decided not to—they were seeing The Great Escape—the urine had dried up. I was steaming rice. I asked if they were hungry and they said no. Your metabolism slows down when you get older, Dad explained. They had shared popcorn at the movie.

[1962 September]

Willie called and said, Do you want to go for a beer? It's a Happening. And I said, Sounds like just going for a beer to me. I heard laughs on the other end of the line. Nah, said Willie, that was the Happening, just calling and asking you to go for a beer. I'm here with Tab, Ron, and the cowpoke twins. All right, I said. Anyway, where do you want to go?

[1962 January]

Meta-happening. Don't count it as my idea but Nell is possessed with the urge to create the Happening and record the Happening at once. The Happening is happening right now. You are witnessing the compression of the type into the paper. Nell is giving me a shoulder massage to loosen me up. Outside the scorpions are sunning themselves on the lawn. Nell is touching my chest. She likes to use her forearms to touch, after her palms. Now she is tkasdgin—sorry— hands incapacitated for a second there—taking my shirt off, as in it is off now. Now she is leaning over me with her nose in my hair rubbing my stomach. She's playing with my waistabdn—waistband—sorry—I know that. Now she's slipping my shorts off onto thef floor and biting my legs. Qhat would be clear to say is I am like—bar e now. Th wind through the window in favor of rushing past me-my—ah—a piece of her hair bruses it and all that—m—and now her tongue ofor the tioahpp ohw I mean. Maybe the HAppening is over or I guess mabe this oneg oes insivble now— invisible sorry—yeah it s mayb an invisble happening no audience—just because tpretty hard to type—wowk

[1963 January]

The idea was we were stranded. We reached out with our oars and scraped the pavement with them and when the boat didn't move we stared at the people walking past and then gazed at each other hopelessly. We're lost, I said. I was at the bow and Nell was at the stern but it didn't matter much because the boat wasn't about to go forward or backward and anyway it was the kind of boat where bow and stern look the same. It had been in Nell's garage and it was a miracle that it wasn't at the bottom of a pond somewhere. Once the fact sank in that we were lost in the middle of the ocean we crawled to each other in the center of the boat and embraced tearfully. A couple of people had stopped to watch by this point, shopping bags in hand. A car pulled up behind us and the driver and passenger got out without seeming to notice that there was a wooden boat taking up the parking space in front of them. When we had looked into one another's eyes for a while we moved back to the bow and stern and returned our long gaze to the street, to the sidewalk, to the stores behind the people. We sat there and drifted. Three books on a desert island, Nell said. *On the Road, The Idiot*, and *Tao Te Ching*. Three foods, I responded. Shrimp cocktail, she said. Just shrimp cocktail? She nodded. We had it settled then. After a while a meter maid came by. Our meter was empty, it turned out. We promised to move but the woman was already scribbling up a ticket. I can feel the waves picking up! Nell hollered. I can feel our luck beginning to change! The meter maid glared at me—I shrugged apologetically—you had to wonder if she hated her uniform as badly as we did—but she couldn't abide Nell, who kept yelling at the sky. She gave up on the ticket, not deigning to waste her time. Better for us, but Nell was offended. We're in the great blue sea, she said, and the sharks swim away from us. Nell, I said, standing in the boat. Being balanced precariously on its center seam, the boat started to wobble. Nell stood too. Soon we were in the street and the boat was wrecked and cars were stopping so they didn't crush us under tire. We decided to repair to my house for a beer. When we came back for the boat it was still there, but righted. Someone had wanted to perpetuate the float.

[1962 June]

Willie gave a reading of the telephone book at The Frog but instead of a telephone book it was a dead cat—no one knows where he got it—Willie has been associated with shady business practices in the past—and instead of reading he looked at its individual hairs and made up addresses. 6127 Teacup Drive. 4222 Callowally Place. P.O. Box 7, New York, New York. He even found one in France, although no one understood because he said it in French, and who could believe that the cat had been all the way there. Still we gave Willie the benefit of the doubt. Then he said the address of the home I grew up in, and no one knows the address of the home I grew up in. My lungs tingled. It was hard to think of home. I thanked God when he finished the reading and passed out drunk next to the pay phones. The Frog had emptied out in the meantime. We took the poor cat home and buried it next to Carl in the backyard, by the mound of sticks and grass. We named it Freckles posthumously.

[1964 September]

Norma had a few drinks at The Frog and declared a Happening. She just stood on the barstool, shouted it, and sat back down. Tom served her a free whiskey and Coke, but I don't know. What was the Happening? You can't just say it and you are already in. But that's what she did. We kept sitting there, talking about the mysteries of marine life. The other patrons stared and stared until they stopped. I should say that Norma is new. Part of the reason she joined us I think is so she could stand on a barstool and declare something. It was all part of the Happening, I guess. Or that's what I told myself.

[1963 April]

We hung a fish on the clothing rack at Fitz's Fine Wear. Well, I did. Shackleton distracted the salesman by asking what kind of suit he should buy to go fishing and I flipped through the rack, all the while slipping a gutted sole out of my coat and tucking it into a gray cotton suit. I don't like any of this, I told Shackleton. Me neither, he said. Of course the salesman had betrayed some dismay that Shack was buying a suit to go fishing in and was more than happy to see us out. He even held the door. His face worried me. Despite the logistics, I suspected that he had never been a child.

[1963 April]

That went so well that we decided to make a day of it. Loma's had fleeced us on the sole so what we did instead is went straight down to the docks. We bought the morning's twelve ugliest fish straight off the captain, took them back to the house, and laid them out on old newspaper on the floor. It was a little gruesome threading coat hangers through the fish and rewinding them into hooks once they were covered in guts but we slipped them into our coats anyway and spent the afternoon shuffling from room to room in the dark house that is Walker-Scott Department Store, enlivening the fineries with marine life. I hung halibut between women's evening gowns. Shackleton placed a rockfish in the pocket of some very sharp business slacks. I dangled a small shark the fishermen had caught—it was a baby, the captain said—they caught a lot of them—in a gap between t-shirts with the names of other cities on them. But our capolavoro was the lobster. Because this one was still living we figured we had to find a good place for it. After some consideration we decided on the shoe rack, where there were hundreds of leather shoes lined up like they knew something we didn't. We put the lobster in the biggest shoe we could find, a size 13 leather clodhopper. You had to believe it would escape before anyone tried the shoe on, but we had a lot of fun imagining a big strong man shrieking when a pair of pincers snipped his toe. On our way past check-out you could already smell the fish settling in. The attendants looked perturbed but didn't seem to know why. We asked if they had any of those fisherman slickers, the ones with the hoods. They didn't. The woman at the register was incensed on our behalf. It was OK, we told her. We were just fishing around.

[1966 May]

Shackleton told me this and although I was not there I feel I should record it. He went to the Oyster House and plunked a telephone down at the place setting in front of him and proceeded to have dinner with the telephone. During some of the dinner, Shackleton said, he picked up the receiver and held a conversation with it about things like the weather, finding work, and the God damned war, but most of the time he just looked into the telephone's eyes. He had exhausted most of his conversational tics with it, had gotten to the point where they were comfortable sitting in silence, which is a point not many of us get to. Still it was a strange night, Shackleton said. The kind of night where the table between you is full of the fullness between you and a person. You want to communicate but at the same time you are very tired of communicating, like a child who has been forced to clear his plate so many times he doesn't know when he's hungry. No—I take that back. Love is not so bad, and Norma is the kind of person I want to paint myself with. But you forget how great a contender time is in the race. It sits there forever, staring at you like a house cat with no plans. Apparently the waiter did not say a word about the telephone but when he brought out the shrimp appetizer, he moved the baby blue base ever so slightly toward the edge of the table to make room for the plate. Shackleton could not decide whether to be angry or to cry out in thanks. As he said, he was having a strange night. When the waiter left, the table's lone candle was laughing at him.

[1965 January]

Norma's friend Mike was sick in the hospital so we told Norma we would see what we could do. The scuba suits were unavailable because Kerry's dad had started acting professional in the last couple years and didn't want his name associated with our antics anymore despite the fact—although we didn't tell him—we should have— that we never carried his sign anyhow. The costume store was charging exorbitant prices and no one had any extra fabric lying around, so in the end we dressed up in Tab's old lab coats and filed through the hospital into Mike's room and surrounded his bed. He was sleeping. We stood there waiting for him to wake up, pretending to be doctors while all the equipment beeped. The thing was nobody had ever done a Happening on request before. After a while Norma went over and shook Mike awake. He took one look around at us and started crying. It was clear right away that we had made a mistake. We were his fear embodied.

[1965 January]

I would probably classify the previous Happening as not-a-Happening simply because of the high functionality quotient. It became clear when Mike woke up and began to cry that we had expected a certain outcome, which was against the spirit of Happenings in general and why we felt so off when Norma asked us to do it. Turns out Mike was on a heavy dose of anesthesia and crying all the time anyway but we didn't know that. I'm not sure it made a difference. What I would classify as a Happening however was when we marched out of there utterly convinced we were doctors. We grinned at the nurses and made concerned faces at the patients passing by. When we made it outside, we passed around the cigarettes that Tab had been harboring in her lab coat. You've never seen so many doctors acting so cheerful together, that's for sure. There were a couple others by the front door eyeing us while we laughed and talked about the different patients we had seen that day. Willie had interrogated a man with an empty eye socket as to the location of his missing eyeball, with no success. Nell fixed a man who had tried to glue himself to his lover. As for Shackleton, he just shook his head. The implication was that he had seen things far worse. Finally he said, Have you ever operated on yourself? One of the doctors by the front door coughed loudly at this and rushed inside. A few minutes later I went back through the hospital to check on Norma, who was still with Mike. That was when the Happening ended, although I forgot to take off my coat. It smelled like a burning house.

[1965 January]

Also not a Happening: Norma on the side of the bed where sick Mike lay, crying herself. Me breaching doctor code—I was still a doctor—it didn't go away for a while—by taking her shoulders and pulling her against my chest. A couple of nurses walked in and were about to say something but I lowered my brows at them. The nurses left and shut the door. Norma's head kept bumping my neck in little sobs. Soon Mike was asleep and Norma was on her feet, contrary to the plan, kissing me.

[1962 March]

Shackleton's rat died which was a real negative until we figured out a plan, which was to take him to the pet store and stand outside and give him a proper funeral. Willie had a trumpet that he brought and played taps. Kerry crocheted him a little beret. We made a felt flag that said Pet Liberation Army and set little Carl up in a dignified position and stood up straight and saluted every once in a while. After a few minutes the pet store owner came out and asked why we were playing taps in front of his establishment. Shackleton, being the bereaved, explained that his rat had died trying to escape its tiny cage and we were doing him the honor he would have wanted. Pet Liberation Army, a customer murmured as she walked into the store. The pet store owner looked at the little flag. I'm going to call the cops, he said. Kerry stared at him like a block of ice. We are the cops, she said. He looked at her for a long time and then at the rat again and back at her. In the end he went inside, making a big show of rolling his eyes. The cops never came. All parties agreed it was a major victory for the Pet Liberation Army. Carl is in our backyard now, beneath a small memorial that consists mainly of sticks and grass. The plan is to watch as he sinks slowly into the earth. Death is just the beginning, Shackleton likes to say. Darkness is just another form of light.

[1964 December]

I have to say there was some malice in it. I flipped over the table and went for his eyes. I didn't actually want to pluck them out or injure Shackleton in any way but once I had my hands on his face I sensed that we were not exactly pretending. It has been a long year. Shackleton kicked me in the stomach with his steel-toed boot and did a somersault over the up-ended table. He stood like a monster from a terrible forest, hunching and widening his arms. By now all the patrons were watching, which was the idea. So few people these days have seen a real bar fight and we wanted to give them something to believe in. I was on my heels when Shackleton rammed my sternum with his head. My spine thumped against the edge of the bar and all the wind went out of me. Then his hand was on my ear, pressing my head to the bar top. For a moment I believed Shackleton really was trying to kill me. As I said, it has been a long year. The confusion with Nell has contributed greatly to a sense of brotherly malevolence growing between us, and the disrepair of the house has grown profound. The larger men in the bar were starting to rise. I held Shackleton around the middle now and was trying my best to flip him onto a table. He was beating my back severely. I won't say either of us liked it. We are not violent people. But it felt good to abuse each other in that squalid, perpetual dimness. We had spent so many nights at The Frog. Finally Shackleton went limp over my shoulder. It was, I saw, because Tom had manifested a shotgun from behind the bar and was aiming it at the two of us. I dropped Shackleton on the floor beside me. His body banged on the hardwood. Everybody flinched, but we were both still alive. I don't know what the fuck has gotten into you, Tom said. We knew Tom. We didn't tip well, but we always tipped. We had met his wife, and little Shirley. You better get out of this bar, he said, before I decorate it with your brains. That seemed a little overdone to me. We weren't even drunk. But Tom was right. We were acting like boys. Shackleton brushed off his jacket and got to his feet slowly. He held his hands in the air. Out, said Tom. I won't say it again. Shack saluted Tom like a rotten pear. Shackleton, Jesus, I said. Let's get out of here. When we got home, we started cleaning the dishes. They were piled halfway to the ceiling, crusted to the point where they had taken on new and alien shapes. Shackleton started at the sink and I started drying. There really were a lot of dishes. Cleaning them was a Happening in itself.

[1968 March]

This one due to authoritarian workings of Norma (just kidding, Norma) who—really though—is right behind me at present dictating, although I'm not listening to her and just writing my own words instead (just kidding again). I try to tell her I don't do these things anymore but she won't have any of it so here goes. We were in the fruit aisle—this is at the grocery store, OK, thanks Norma—and the pineapples were right next to the bananas and one of us got the idea—OK, it was me, I'll take the credit, even though it wasn't really a Happening, I was just messing around—fine, it's a Happening, everything's a Happening, sure—and put the banana across the bottom of the pineapple like a mouth and took a couple small tomatoes, since they were adjacent, and put them on top of the pineapple where the green spiny part stuck out. Not much to it. Oh.

Except the nose. (Don't forget the nose, says Norma.) There was a nose too, a green bean Norma found all the way in the vegetable aisle. In the end the pineapple looked like a big-faced man. We left it there. That was all. OK—Norma reminds me that it was funny. It was funny. That's true. We are going to go make breakfast now. With a different pineapple. One without a face. It is a March spring morning. It's all happening. Get it? Happening? Also funny, Norma says. The birds kept us up last night, chirping. Or maybe it was us who kept them up.

Note added later due to non-Happening quality of previous

Of course Happenings can happen anywhere and any way but under duress is not the proper way to engage in or record. I don't know. It just didn't feel right. A fruit face? If a fruit face is a Happening, what isn't? Our whole history would be kaput.

[1961 February]

We went to the park and played a whole baseball game
without ball, gloves, or bat. Shackleton pitched and Nell
stood in the batter's box adjusting her imaginary balls.
When he let fly she swung in slow motion and her eye-
lids widened as she felt the crack of the bat and Kerry,
who was standing in the outfield, began to chase the
ball toward the home run fence (there was no fence, just
a drainage ditch) with her hand stretched out behind
her. When she hit the ditch she leapt and landed with
her hand held inches above the grass and lay there until
the rest of the fielders, me and Willie and the cowpoke
twins, ran up to her and asked whether she had the
ball or not. Of course she had the ball. She showed it
to us like it was a diamond she had dug out of a mine
wall. All right, all right, we said, just checking. The next
inning Shackleton pegged one of the cowpoke twins

with a pitch and in an instant the benches were cleared, the cowpoke twins charging Shack with the imaginary bat. I threw my body on top of Shackleton's to protect him but the cowpoke twins were relentless and before long we were fleeing to the drainage ditch and chucking clods of dirt over the rim to protect ourselves. This was about the time when the little league team arrived with their uniforms and their clean black bat bags and one of the coaches came up and asked if they could use the field. We had been waiting for this. Just one more inning, Shackleton told them with poise, crawling out of the ditch and wiping off his pants. Kerry and Nell and the cowpoke twins settled into their positions and I strolled to the plate. I felt the weight of the world on me. The whole little league team was watching wondering what in hell we were doing so I knew I had to hit a big one to prove it to them. Shackleton looked to first. Looked to third. Then he wound up—his limbs were like flamingos—like windmill blades—and sent a heater at me, right over the plate. I squeezed my eyes shut and swung as hard as I could. Heard the clop of the ball into the catcher's mitt. The almost silent buzz of relief in the field. I looked at my bat like it had done me wrong. Strike one! I called to the fielders. They punched their mitts and got down in athletic position. But I'll be damned. I couldn't put bat on ball. It was those kids staring me down from the sidelines ready to take over. On strike three I jumped in front of the pitch just to get on base. You can almost see the bruise.

[1961 March]

Soccer wasn't the same. We eyed the ball like it was salvation but no one could agree on where it was. Kerry kicked Shackleton in the shin and he went down hard, extending his groaning time to the outer limits of human sympathy. We ended up kicking the ball around like a pack of sweat bees while Shack howled and watched the swelling rise. Nell tackled me into the grass. She whispered unmentionable things in my ear about what we would do to each other on the field in the case of victory. I took that as a challenge. The ball leapt up with a life of its own and began to run laps around the sideline. I followed as close behind as I could.

[1960 August]

The creative process is a strange one: we covered ourselves in white paint and walked out into the street. We had been painting the front porch was all. Shackleton missed and spread a stroke along my forearm. It felt good. The paint was cold and wet and clotted on my skin. Some drops had already hardened on him, too, from splashes out of the paint bucket. We looked at each other. It didn't take long. Then we walked down to the drugstore to pick up a few beers although what we were really doing was just being white. We had to seize the few moments before the paint hardened our limbs, while we still had a chance to show it off. In the end Leland wouldn't sell us a six-pack anyway. He thought we were drunk. We had forgotten about the paint fumes. They stone you out of your mind.

[1970 March]

Well. When I was at the newspaper I got a call from Kerry saying her brother had been drafted. We are of course in the cold grip of war and Oscar had gotten the letter detailing that he had to go down and submit himself to testing to ascertain whether he was worthy of being forced to fight and I told Kerry to stop, Shackleton and I would handle it, seeing as we were too old to die for our country. She was in tears. She thanked me. Then I called Shackleton and we made a plan. We met at the recruiting center, a barracks in the shoreside sun. You expected it to carry a gray cloud over it but men with short hair kept walking in and out as if nothing sinister were inside. Shackleton and I did our duty. We went in. I held my hand out to the officer, who had wide cheeks on top of a body that was nothing but gristle, and he shook my hand and told me promptly

that I had to wait while they took care of my friend.
Yes sir, I said. My friend, Oscar Polk, he loves this God
damned war. I patted Shackleton on the back. The
officer looked at me and looked at Shackleton's long
hair. His eyes were narrow. Glad to hear that, he said.
He'll tell you himself, I said. Shackleton nodded sol-
emnly. A low growl began in the bottom of his throat.
His shoulders rose and his eyes grew wide. The growl
was louder now and escalating into a screech when
finally he quieted. I translated. He says he would like
to go to the war, I said. He says he hates the Viet Cong
and loves the American way and hates Communism.
He loves napalm—I looked at Shackleton—you love
napalm?—he nodded vigorously—loves napalm and
would like to go over there as soon as possible. Sir.
Shackleton had his hands held together as if in prayer.
The officer, when you really looked at him, couldn't
have been much older than us. I should really call my
captain, he said. I think you two are trying to pull a fast
one. He picked up the black telephone receiver on the
intake desk. Sir! I just about shouted. I quieted myself.
Sir. Here we have a citizen who wants to go to war for
his country. Don't tell me you aren't going to let him go.
This is a man—but now the officer was looking past

me. I followed his eyes. Shackleton was frothing at the mouth. He hunched and glared maniacally. The ceiling lights were blinking rapidly and Shack was starting to shake with them, bouncing in his trousers. I ran to catch him just as he dove onto the floor. Doctor! the officer was yelling. An older man rushed out from behind a baby blue curtain with an ear light in his hand. I let Shack down to the tile as he writhed. My friend, I shouted. He wants to fight the war! Shackleton was pounding on the floor now, and the doctor leapt to help me pin down his arms. For a second I thought Shack wasn't faking it. He looked old, almost gray at the temples. It has been two years since we moved out of the house on Celso Street and he works at an ice cream shop now and that's all he talks about when we talk, how the customers are base in their desires and can't take a joke and worst of all are averse to experimentation in terms of toppings. You're all settled down, he likes to say, which isn't true. I have a job at the newspaper setting type and even doing a little design and this allows me material means such as a car and the kind of treats that the patrons of the ice cream shop are looking for when they go to visit Shackleton, but that doesn't mean I settled. I have Norma. She's what I have. Shackleton screeched and shuddered. His fist whacked the doctor hard in the chest but the doctor appeared unaffronted, so absorbed was he in trying to calm my friend. You know, I told the doctor, I think he's ready to fight. I hoped Shack would hear me and get the idea that it was time to slow it down. But he kept fighting the ground, calming only gradually and lashing out every once in a while to show he wasn't done with the throes. I made eyes at the doctor. He really wants to fight, I said. The doctor's brows went low. No. He shook his head gravely. Oh no, he said. Gently the doctor placed his hand in the center of Shack's chest. Then he stood and went over to the intake officer and whispered some things, waving his hand over the sheet of paper where OSCAR EDWARD POLK was printed in blue mimeograph. The officer nodded. You could see he wanted to object, but the doctor was vehement. I chanced a glance at Shack. His eyes were open. He winked at me. I kicked him in the side and started to cry, I really did. It wasn't fake or a Happening or anything. It was just that windowless building filled with the rhythms of boys who were going to pass their tests and get sent off to war where their vital signs weren't going to mean anything. We were both very near to and very far from the fight. The doctor turned and saw me crying. Shaking his head, he walked back behind the baby blue curtain. The intake officer glared at us. Well, boys, he said. You got off this time. I saw Shackleton open his mouth and think better of it and instead stand up wearily—a real weariness—something I had never seen in him—and go over and shake the officer's hand. The officer took his palm with surprise. He shook and shook, and only after a long time did Shackleton let go of him. Outside, the sun and shore were waiting for us. We did a good thing, I said. Shack nodded at nothing. He was looking above him, where a seagull, rat of the sky, soared. His words had flown away.

[1962 October]

Like children, we played at war. A blanket fortress. Machine gun hands. The day outside was a rare gray so we army-crawled around the house trying to catch sight of each other's boots. Halfway through I was sure I got Shackleton, pegged his head with a pillow grenade when he poked it out of the kitchen. It was a dud! he yelled from behind the wall. I'm still alive! Bullshit you are! I yelled back. I scrambled for all the pillows in the room, sticking my hand into no man's land to get a last cushion. Marty's 70th, it said. I holed up behind the couch pulling all the firepower tight to my body while we waited each other out. Then there was a knock. We'd forgotten. We'd asked Kerry over for a beer to whittle by the cloudy day. Still clinging to my guns I stood and opened the door. Kerry looked strangely at me, either for the pillows I held or for the blood in my eyes on a Saturday afternoon. I opened my mouth to explain but a war cry rang out from the kitchen and Shackleton sprinted across the rug with an armful of oranges, not having intuited that a truce was cast by the fact of Kerry's arrival. You could see he was struggling to throw the oranges because he was using both arms to hold them so when he got close enough to us he just lunged, letting his arms fall in front of him, and the oranges cascaded onto the floor and rolled to our feet. They sat there useless, cluttering the hardwood in our little foyer. Kerry was holding a six-pack of beer, I saw. A peace offering. She held it out. I got you, Shackleton said. He was on his knees wheezing. It's over Shack, I said. No one wins. I put down my pillows and took the beer and walked into the living room. Some of the oranges had strayed there. Shackleton looked shocked when I picked one up and threw it to Kerry. She began to peel its skin back. It was as ripe as the evening sun.

[wink wink]

Dear Guy Guy,

Once we went to the drive-in and you massaged my neck for an hour and I was like a lightning bug, you could have seen me light up from across the lot! Which probably ruined the movie for everyone although it was Doctor Zhivago and we were all tired out by that anyway.

A little surprise for you...

Love and kisses,

You-Know-Who.[*]

------

[*] This entry, along with the others by my mother, was handwritten with blue pen in her trademark slanted cursive.

A NOTE TO FUTURE LOOKERS-IN

Contributions to the Rolodex are strictly limited to the author of the Rolodex. Content is also strictly limited to real Happenings, whether composed or improvisational. Seriously, Norma, please don't write in here. Thank you for the surprise and everything but Jesus. We have to have some space to ourselves. Please?

[1963 August]

We began digging up a shrub in a strip of soil off Broadway. No one reacted the way we'd hoped. People just walked by. They thought we were city workers, when we were really archeologists looking for remnants of a lost civilization beneath the tangled root system of the shrub. After a while we got to the bottom and pulled the plant out. Still nobody stopped. People stopping was not the idea but I did feel it was sad for the Happening to be reduced by inattention so I got down on my knees and scraped in the hole with my fingernails looking for something. There wasn't much to be found given that the hole was surrounded by city streets but finally I grasped a hard object, a chunk of sidewalk concrete that had gotten buried there. I pulled it free. Brushed the soil from it. Rose to my knees and held it with a glow of mystery. Shackleton bent to gaze at the chunk. I think it's a—I think it's a— I whispered. Willie took it in his hands. Hallelujah! he shouted. Finally a couple people looked at us. Hallelujah! he shouted again. But it didn't feel right. The cars and pedestrians were whipping by and it was only the yelling that got their attention. Anyone could see that Willie was holding a piece of broken concrete to the sky and trying to find a glint in it. He kept shouting. Hallelujah! After a minute I had to tell him to quiet down. We didn't want to share our archeological find with the hoi polloi before it was registered with the Smithsonian, I said, but my heart wasn't even in that. The people roaring past were fine without us. Quietly, we put the chunk of concrete and the shrub back where they had been and kicked the soil into place with the sides of our boots. On the way home we stopped at The Frog. Tom asked about our dirty fingernails. Been working today, have you, boys? We shrugged. It was a little embarrassing really. It's possible that it is time to go out and get a job.

[1963 September]

We tried at least. Shackleton wrote HAPPENINGS $1 on a piece of plywood and we went and hung around by the boardwalk. Willie stood next to me with a pitcher of water and Shackleton slouched next to him looking sour. When we got a customer Willie would hand them the pitcher and we would all stand and wait. The idea was that they could wash their hands in the water or dump it on the ground or pour it on Shackleton's head, which was why he was there. We had provided the tools for the Happening and the rest was up to them. No one understood. We only had three customers and one was a little kid who couldn't reach high enough to pour water on Shackleton's head even if he wanted to. Shack bent down, but the kid just tried to drink out of the pitcher. We had to grab it out of his hand. The water was salt water from the ocean. The kid's dad—a square—the kind of square who thinks he's not a square—asked for his money back. The other two customers were a pair of high school girls who poured the water on each other's feet. Admittedly it was a hot day but they were not our preferred clientele. Once they got ahold of the pitcher they pretended like we weren't even there. They handed me a five when the pitcher was empty. No one had change. They shrugged and looked at each other, then swayed away like they had thrown the bill in the ocean.

[1972 October]

The marriage was technically a Happening so I feel obliged to record it here. It has been a long time. Shackleton is still around although his hair is a lot longer and Nell managed to come too but Willie is dead, Kerry has disappeared, and most of the others we've lost track of. Norma has basically forgotten about the Happenings—standing on a barstool at The Frog for instance—or even her days with Mike at the hospital—but I got to thinking about it and decided it was going to be a Happening. Not the wedding but the entire marriage. That it was never going to STOP happening. This might be off-putting if you forget that we were never pretending at the Happenings, we were just being, that it was never a joke to us, it was just life. So the rest of the marriage is supposed to be that kind of being, and Norma's eye rolls are part of it, and so are the chairs stacked on the lawn this morning, and Shackleton's terrible tuxedo, and the ring I bought that was one tier lower than what Norma wanted, and the wet grass that is ruining all of our shoes. The vows are scheduled for five o'clock which is a nice conservative time and that will be the beginning of the Happening and the end will be when one of us dies. I can't help looking at Nell and thinking of some of the times we used to have. Was that me in them? I hardly know that Guy. Still I see the straight life as easier to abide if you think of it as one long project instead of as an extended shrug. The other option is Shackleton. He's gone a different way. Art lives forever but it also kills its elders and every time he calls with another story about a public disrobing or a manhole cover removal I hear him one step closer to the outside of the circle and I look around at the representation-alist paintings on our walls and they don't look so bad. We've been gifted multiple sets of knives today, I just know it. I'll make sure to use them all. Diced carrots, radish discs, an apple open and browning. This is how we begin our lives.

[1965 April]

An accident with a knife... Easter morning...[*]

All it takes is intention...

---

[*] What you don't see here is a fan of brown blood wiped across the card. My father must have cut himself with a knife while preparing Easter breakfast and taken the opportunity to revive his flagging Rolodex.

[1964 February]

We hauled a bed into Horton Plaza and lay in it, Nell
and I. In our bedclothes. Me underwear, her nothing.
That's how she sleeps. The idea was that it was three
in the afternoon and in the light people would get to
see the strangeness of sleeping but instead a crowd
gathered on Nell's side of the bed simply because she
was naked. My eyes were closed. I was trying to dream.
But she saw all those people and I could feel her body
begin to sweat. Under our thin sheet—a single, white
sheet—it was too hot for anything more—she turned to
me and planted her lips on my lips. You could hear the
crowd inhale. She kissed me harder then. I felt a little
strange. Then she climbed on top of me and started
massaging me with her hand and I hoped the crowd
couldn't tell if that was actually what she was doing or
if we were just pretending. She slipped her hand under

my briefs, and for a second I forgot that we were in the middle of Horton Plaza being watched by a crowd of people. But then I opened my eyes to the sun that was shining down along with the many faces and became aware that Nell was playing for the crowd and not for me. I pulled her ear to me and whispered, Maybe the Happening is over. She shook her head. She leapt on top of me and although I was aware that it was not really me she was moving around on top of—it was really the people watching her—she was really fucking them—I couldn't help it and in a few minutes I came which felt like the day bursting out of me and absorbing the faces of the astonished crowd and trying to expel them at once. Once I had done that I felt a deep hollowness. Nell collapsed in my arms and curled against my body again, and because the Happening was still technically in effect we resumed pretending it was night. Until word of the police began to circulate and Willie and Shack and Kerry who were waiting in the wings swept into the square and carried the bed to Kerry's truck and Kerry hit the gas, us still on the mattress, the wind washing over us from the top of the cab. It was like a dream. I felt very distant. Nell luxuriated in the sweeping air and pulled the sheet off of herself. I could see Shack looking back at her in the rearview mirror and Kerry shaking her head. We were so covered in life, but I felt and still feel a little dead after the feat.

[1964 October]

Happenings should not have victims. Should not have a man-worm wriggling at the end of a hook. Or a sun being slowly eclipsed. Or the groans of sexual satisfaction leaking through the slats of your own house when you return from the first day of your first job in years only to turn out to be the groans of your lover whose body you have held in your arms, whose boat you have rowed across the pavement of the city. Sure there was never any agreement. Sure love is free. But wrapped in towels, bandanas over their eyes? To truncate touch, limit it to the sex? Shackleton's moral compass is a stick lying in the dirt. I can't account for Nell. Sure we have been growing apart. But I cannot forget standing frozen at the threshold with my new briefcase in hand, watching two half-mummified people crawling over each other's nakedness. One of them with my heart wrapped up in her hand. Record it, Nell said, laughing. Get the typewriter out. Or join. All the windows were open. There was no shame. There should be no shame in this palm tree world but I am sorry, there is. The walls were vibrating. I knew that something vital had left us here.

Introductory Remarks

Shackleton comes back from New York wearing a straw hat. He stands at the arrivals gate and presses his hands together and holds them straight above his head. Praise the metal bird, he says. Praise the sky. Shack? I say. Guy, he says. Happenings.

Outside I start up Kerry's truck and Shack gets into the ripped up bucket seat and starts to tell me about what they are doing at Rutgers. Rutgers? I say. New Jersey, he says. I thought you were in New York? And he explains that the new art is just being. Being? Shack nods. This is art, he says, holding his hands out. Those three clouds. The stewardesses waiting for the bus. See that gate? If we sat cross-legged on the pavement and waited for it to speak to us. Art. Flash your lights. A Happening.[*]

____

[*] It is hard to know which Happening Shackleton

You just do things? I ask. He yawns. You just do things.

I downshift to get up to speed for the highway. The on-ramp is covered in a thin sheet of sand. I love to paint, Shackleton says. But what I love more is to be.

We need to tell Kerry this, I say. We need to tell everyone.

When we drop off the truck, Kerry wonders what took us so long. Life, we say. Art. Shackleton still has on his straw hat. I have an idea, he says.

So do I.

I hereby inaugurate this Rolodex.

---

encountered in New Jersey. Though Allan Kaprow was a faculty member at Rutgers at the time, his most famous works took place in New York City—the first, "18 Happenings in 6 Parts," about a year before Shackleton's visit. Most likely Shackleton was involved in one of the smaller-scale, undocumented events that formed an early cornerstone of the Fluxus movement.

[sorry!]

Dear Guy,

Sorry! Had thought that maybe leaving the Rolodex lying all over the house was an invitation of sorts but maybe not. I won't write in it again!

Oh wait, I already am...

Love is too stout to hold back! What can I do!

A thousand kisses,

The Woman You Love, Who Promises Never To Write In Your Rolodex Again Till Death Do Us Part

POINT TAKEN

OK, I won't leave the Rolodex out anymore. But please could you just PRETEND that you haven't flipped through and read everything? God, I hope you didn't read everything. It's dumb, that's all. It's nothing. Just let it be.

[don't be so hard on yourself]

I think it's beautiful, sweetie.

*****

NORMA!! For Christ's sake!

I'm serious.

This is not for you.

[1965 August]

A miracle in disguise: on the way to Mom and Dad's, I passed through Grand Central Station. A man with a beard saw my beard and told me to wait around. Something was going to happen, he said. My ears pricked up at the word happen but I couldn't believe anything in the nature of our Happenings was going to take place. Then again it was going to be a while before my train and the simple presence of so many souls gave me a feeling of great potential, so I waited around. After a while I noticed three look-alike figures being led by their hands from different corners of the station. They were wrapped in cloth, blindfolded by it. The figures converged at the information booth at the center of the station, the people who had led them left, and the figures started calling out names. A small crowd gathered. Some passers-by made a point to walk quickly in the opposite direction as I have learned is a main component of most Happenings but other people—mostly the freaky ones—the ones with beards, like me, and hair—started to gather around the cloth-covered figures, who were now beginning to unwrap themselves while still calling out. One of them was a young man with his own beard and two of them were young women, although I don't know why I call them young. They were only a couple years younger than me. The cloth came slowly off and you could see they were wearing jeans and t-shirts underneath the way anyone would. Soon you could hardly believe that they had been escorted into Grand Central Station wrapped in cloth except for the pile of discarded rags at their feet. That was when they gave themselves to a great silence, glanced around, and walked away in three different directions. People with huge cameras photographed them. I watched the man disappear into his own stride until he stopped suddenly at one of the payphones that dotted the floor of the station. He put a dime into it and picked up the receiver. He stood for a long time like that. Longer than any normal conversation would take, and he wasn't even talking. Then he hung up and walked away. The bearded guy who had told me to wait around was still standing next to me. He made noises of awe. I felt his elbow nudge me. Tomorrow they're going to go into the woods and call each other's names again. I looked at him. Sorry? They're going to hang upside down from tarps, he said. He was eager, I could see, the type of person who gathers his information third-hand. Who's in charge? I asked the man. He looked at me in disbelief. Kaprow, he almost whispered. As if speaking of a deity. Then he took my forearm in his palm and squeezed. Who are you? he asked. My name is Guy Sutter, I said. He nodded, the bearded man. And clapped me on the shoulder before he walked away. I'm sure you'll be fine, he said. You had to notice, though, that the lighting in Grand Central Station hadn't changed an iota. Suddenly—and I hadn't even been home yet—there was iced tea and a sunset waiting for me at my parents' new house—I wanted to return to San Diego and lie down spread eagle in the middle of the street. Feel the pavement on my back, the threat of loose cars hovering above me. We were just beginning, I told myself. But I already felt like I had come to the end.[*]

---

[*] The Happening my father describes is almost undoubtedly the first installment of Allan Kaprow's "Calling," which took

place on August 21, 1965, a Saturday. Because Kaprow's Happenings were so few and far between, it would have been a stroke of almost incomprehensible fortune for him to have stumbled upon one by chance. At times I doubt his naïveté; I wonder whether, even from across the country, he had heard word of the approaching Happening and timed his visit home to intersect with it, recording the event with an improvisatory air for the sake of effect.

Curiously, while photographs of the event depict a crowd similar to the one my father describes gathering around the performers at Grand Central Station, Allan Kaprow subtitled "Calling" "A Happening for performers only." My father doesn't appear in the photographs, although I have searched for him. There are many faceless men in the crowd.

[1965 September]

I got back to San Diego and lay down spread eagle in the middle of the street. The effect was compromised because Norma insisted on standing next to me and directing traffic, but in the end she was probably right that if she hadn't I would have been crushed under tire. I don't know. There was something about me that wanted to touch everything, have the heavy pavement hold me tight. I lay face-up and looked at the sky. The asphalt gets so hot out here it burned my arms. Still I was happy as I lay there feeling. What you don't realize is how clean the street stays, tires sandblasting it minute after minute. When I got up I felt clean. Burned, but clean.

[1963 February]

For once we wanted people to know that what we were doing was art. So Shackleton played the clarinet—his parents got it for him when he was a child—he was never higher than fourth chair, he says, and you can sure tell—and I pretended to drown. We stood on the sidewalk just outside of Walker-Scott. It was Wednesday so there wasn't a lot of traffic but I got plenty of looks just by holding my breath and waving my arms frantically. Seeing that, most shoppers scuttled away. Between my sinking and Shackleton's clarinet squeaks they thought we had lost it, though we had planned the Happening out beforehand on a piece of notebook paper. Diagrams and a climax where I sucked the water into my lungs. But it was hard to drown. In the end a nicely dressed man came out of the department store and took me by the shoulders and said calmly: I'm a doctor. For a second I was relieved. Finally someone who understood. Then I realized that he proposed to save me. I said no—I was fine—it was just art—but after he left, it took me an hour to get all the air back into my body. The walk home was long and windy. I only remember the parts (there were a lot of them) where I almost blacked out, my brain trying to pull the oxygen north. Back at the house hot toddies were the order of the day, although winter here is no winter at all. Hell, the water had almost overcome me. I needed to warm from the inside out.

[1963 November]

Today John Fitzgerald Kennedy was shot. Nell was over and Kerry was over and after a while Willie was over and even the cowpoke twins and Ron and Tab. The TV played and played. Someone said what if we had some kind of funeral, go out in the street. But the President hadn't been dead even 24 hours. It wasn't right. Then Willie said unthinkably that we might re-enact the shooting. Blow his brains out in the backyard. He went on. Nobody stopped him. I can be the killer, he said, and Guy can be the President. Do you still have that little wagon? he asked, looking at me, looking at Shackleton. It took him that long to realize how off he was. The passion had gone out of our bodies sentences ago. All we could do the rest of the day was sprawl about the house brooding. Someone put on Peter, Paul and Mary. What I'll always remember is how the second a side ended, someone was there to flip the record right away. You didn't get a lick of silence. Then for the third time Where Have All the Flowers Gone played. The trio sang, Oh, when will they ever learn? and the needle rose. The room was suddenly a headache. I sprang up and nearly scratched the record trying to get the voices back. Peter, Paul and Mary were ghostlike, three jilted lovers, but they were all we had. God, I wanted so badly to create something. But the day just piled on.

...[*]

---

[*] The last Rolodex card consists only of the above: an ellipsis, no date included. My father might have typed it any time between the spring of 1960 and the day he died. I feel certain, however, that the ellipsis was set down between 1974, the last dated entry, and 1980, the year of my birth. He knew something was waiting for him.

The Rolodex Photographs

The story goes: Two weeks before I was born, my father went out and bought an orange Volkswagen convertible.

By that time, my parents had lived in St. Louis for five years. Realizing his gig at the Evening Tribune would never support a family, my father had found a managerial job halfway across the country, at the St. Louis Post-Dispatch. Now he and my mother owned a house in an up-and-coming suburb and, when they learned my mother was pregnant, they even invested in a brand-new wood-paneled station wagon. Stability was comfortable. Wonderful, even. The dreams of my father's young life seemed to be leaving him.

Then, as I imagine it, he returned to the Rolodex. He found this photograph.

He had taken it, my mother said, just before they met. My father had been camping with his friends when an orange Beetle pulled up beside Kerry's truck. Overcome by a sudden feeling of familiarity, my father took a picture of it and tucked it into his Rolodex. His first car, he told himself, would be just like it.

Sixteen years later the photo struck him. Agitated, he left the house. My mother, who was eight months pregnant, didn't know where he had gone. She was on the verge of calling the police when he zipped up the driveway.

He was behind the wheel of an orange 1980 Volkswagen Cabriolet. They no longer sold Beetles, but the convertible looked almost like a bug, if you imagined hard enough. My mother ran outside when she heard its radio buzzing in the driveway. My father stood on the seat grinning, elbows resting on the rollbar. She had an instant to decide whether to be horrified or to indulge him.

When he drove her around the neighborhood in the new car, she says, he drove carefully. He knew where the line was. The line was me.

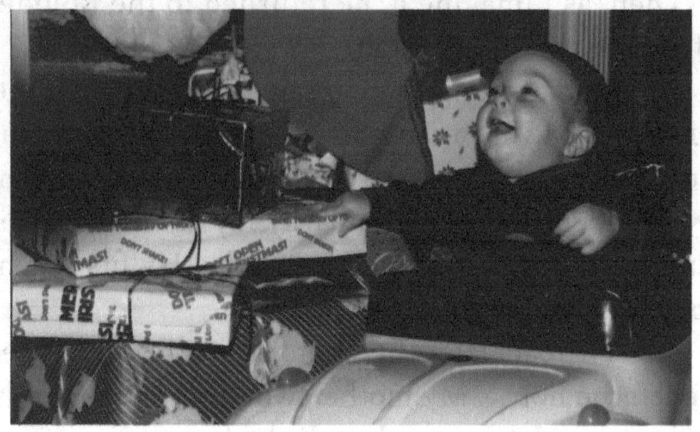

The story also goes: My first Christmas, my father bought a Volkswagen Beetle.

It was two feet wide, three feet long, and cream pink. My father hoisted me into the driver's seat and I banged the horn with both hands.

The horn didn't honk. But when I moved forward a few inches and rattled the ornaments on the tree, I imagine my father was overcome—with tenderness, with a brief flash of envy, with awe at the life in which he'd found himself.

The pink Beetle sat in our playroom long after I had outgrown it. It never occurred to me to wonder who they were keeping it for, or, when it finally disappeared, to ask what it felt like to throw it away.

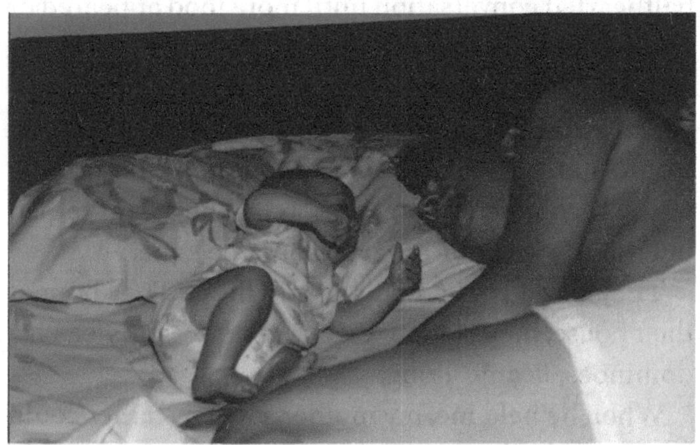

Before they moved to St. Louis, my parents lived together in San Diego for six years. Once a month, my mother tells me, Shackleton would come over for dinner. After they ate, Shackleton and my father would repair to the front porch for beers. My father would rise when it got late, predicting a long next day at the Evening Tribune, and shake Shackleton's hand before returning inside.

As the years went by, my mother says, Shackleton began to arrive earlier for dinner. He spoke less and less, and he ate more and more ravenously. What started as a celebration of the past grew into a ritual wherein my mother and father watched Shackleton quietly devour the food they offered him. He would then make halfhearted conversation until more food appeared or my father offered to accompany him to the porch.

Soon my father began to return inside after a single beer. My mother waited on the couch. Together they would stare at Shackleton's silhouette, still outlined in the rocking chair on the porch. They went to bed uneasily. By the morning he would be gone.

They moved to St. Louis as if in flight. They bought their house, their station wagon, and the Cabriolet. Like dominoes, I came along.

When he held me, my mother says, my father could not stop grinning.

One night, my mother says, my father fell asleep next to me on the bed. She carried me to my crib. When she returned to lie on the mattress beside him, he woke and stared at her as if she were me. She had never seen such wonder in him.

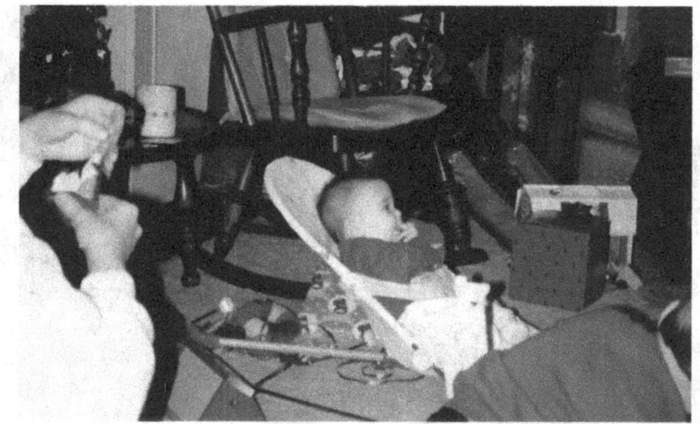

My brother Bob was born less than two years later. Did Dad get tired? Did the Christmas presents pile up like dirty dishes on Celso Street? Wonder has a limit, and at that limit it changes. Maybe it becomes belief.

I remember the year when Bob played a Wise Man in our school's Christmas pageant. He was hardly old enough to remember a line. But after the show, my father named every detail of his performance: Bob's reverent stride toward the manger, his gaze upon the child, his careful grip on the myrrh. Bob listened fiercely and grinned when my father tousled his hair. That was the first time it occurred to me that for all he had gained in us, my father had also lost something. It filled the air around us.

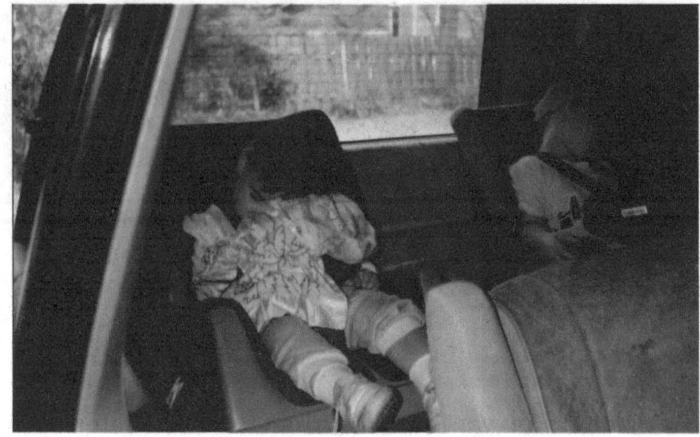

A normal Saturday morning: My mother made pancakes shaped like the first letters of our names. Small *g* for me, large *G* for my father. We ate until the batter ran out.

Then came "quiet time," two hours when we had to go to our rooms and play by ourselves. I was a shy kid, absorbed in books until the hours were up. My brother, who could not stand silence, made up plays.

Finally the knock on the door came. My brother sprinted down the stairs and leapt into the station wagon while I followed behind. My father drove us to Ted Drewes Frozen Custard. Even in summer, wooden icicles hung from the edge of the roof.

I ordered a Lemon Crumb Sundae. Bob ordered a Fox Treat Concrete. My father always ordered with panache: Southern Delight with a touch of Terramizzou. Or part Brennan Blend, part Crater Copernicus, ratio to be determined by whoever was scooping the custard. Some days he would even order a Sutter Special, which involved ever-changing combinations of Butterscotch, Cindermint, Tart Cherry, Tedads, and Whipped Cream mixed using elaborate strategies my father prescribed. "Don't worry," he'd say to our server. "It'll be just right the way you make it."

Afterward we would go to the park, where my father chased us in circles until we collapsed. On the way home, Bob and I invariably fell asleep in the back seat of the car.

As we grew older, we took fewer trips to Ted Drewes. At fifteen, I drove there to get my license hours. At sixteen, I'd ask Mom, "Does Dad want to go to Ted Drewes tomorrow?" She'd say, "You know he likes to do that with you." I would get my old Sundae out of duty. Bob had already gone his own way by then, so he would be in the theater for the weekend or gathering at a show with his friends.

But in the photo, it is a normal Saturday. Maybe even

one of the first. We are asleep in our driveway, where my father won't wake us. He will let us sleep, and when we wake up, we will wonder for a short but fevered moment where we are.

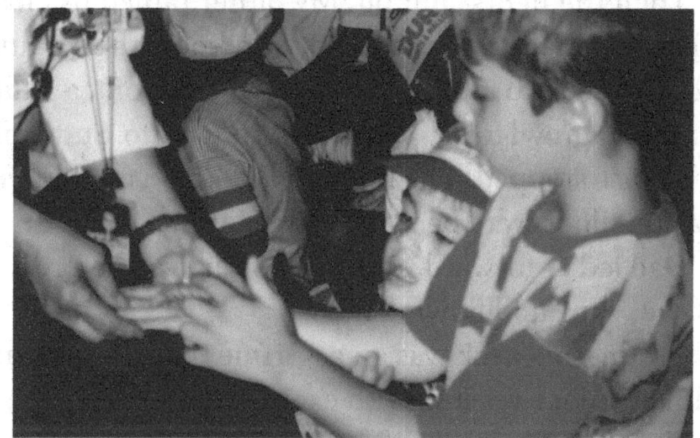

One Saturday, however, we didn't go to the park after Ted Drewes. With an air of mystery, my father took a left out of the parking lot instead of right. We sat in the car longer than we were used to. The scenery grew unfamiliar. Turns piled on turns. Finally we arrived in a wide parking lot dotted with cars.

My father held our hands as we crossed the lot toward a low institutional building. Inside the building's two steel doors was a gymnasium. At the front of the gymnasium was a long line of men dressed in white cloaks. Some people were seated on the hardwood floor. We sat too. There was an awkward silence. I remember looking at my father, who seemed rapt. He didn't tell us what was happening.

Then the lights shut off. My father pulled us close. The men began to mumble, and soon their mumbling grew into a din. A rustling at the front, a ritual action. A growl followed by a sharp falsetto. Suddenly the noise stopped. The few of us gathered on the gymnasium floor were beckoned to the front.

Dad led us forward. Together, we arrived before one of the white and flowing men.

Around his neck was an assortment of trinkets and junk. His face was red with exertion.

He said: "The body of you." Then he took my hand and placed it in my own mouth. I took it out. The man seemed sorry. From his pocket, he produced a gummy worm and placed it in my hand.

A camera flashed, my brother gripped my arm, and we filed back to our spot on the gymnasium floor. That was when the lights started flashing. My brother began to whimper, and I could see the progression of my father's face in the strobe: First eager, then intent, then distracted, concerned, worried, regretful. A rapid-heartbeat soundtrack had started up and the men were dancing deliriously. Bob was crying now. My father stood. He took our hands and led us out of the gym.

On the way home, my father did not speak. His

silence turned into a fierce resignation.

We did not fall asleep in the car on the way back, and we did not tell Mom about the Happening when we returned. Maybe we understood: It was over, it didn't need words. My father had put it to rest.

Soon afterward, my father left for Italy. The conference was an opportunity to learn about European newspaper design, but more importantly it gave him the chance to ride a moped from Tuscany to Calabria. The conference brochure had advertised the trip as an improbable add-on. Believing he needed it, my mother convinced him to go.

While he was gone, my mother took us to the pool every day. She paid us a dollar to wash the Volkswagen in the driveway. She led us through the Natural History Museum, where an artificial ice cave echoed with recorded drips and ended with a life-sized mammoth. Overcome by its sad, giant eyes, I convinced myself the mammoth was not a replica but a real animal that had been buried beneath St. Louis and unearthed intact.

Meanwhile my father reached Pompei, where Mt. Vesuvius's smoke still rose into the air. He braced against the roadside lava for a photograph.

Stuck to the back of the photograph was this ticket:

"In this Sanctuary
I prayed for You."

I can't imagine my father praying, but I can't imagine him passing up the opportunity either. Did he pray for me, Bob, and Mom? For Shackleton, who he hadn't seen since moving to St. Louis, whose letters arrived less and less frequently? Could he have prayed for Kerry? Tab? Willie? Was lighting a candle a Happening?

If his prayer was a Happening, it was the last of its kind. He had Italy, the open road, the perfectly preserved past. What did it matter? We were on our green street back in St. Louis waiting for him.

I believe it was then that my father understood *we* were the Happening. Our home, our ordinary life. The only thing he had to do was return to us.

When he returned, my father pulled his suitcase from the airport taxi and set it on the lawn. He hugged me, picked up Bob, and kissed my mother. Then he bent to Dolly, the fountain my mother had grown up with in her own yard, and whispered something in her ear. He whispered for a long time, and of course Bob and I begged him to tell us what he had told her.

He wouldn't say, and Dolly wouldn't tell us either. She ran all summer, and finally I understood that the words were water. They poured and poured again.

It seems clear to me now that my father was letting go of art in favor of life. Strangely, Allan Kaprow enacted a similar transition in his own Happenings.

By the mid-eighties Kaprow was simply brushing his teeth. He described it like an artist who had already achieved his apotheosis:

I would be alone in my bathroom, without art spectators. There would be no gallery, no critic to judge, no publicity. This was the crucial shift that removed the performance of everyday life from all but the memory of art. I could, of course, have said to myself, "Now I'm making art!!" But in actual practice, I didn't think much about it.

My awareness and thoughts were of another kind. I began to pay attention to how much this act of brushing my teeth had become routinized, nonconscious behavior, compared with my first efforts to do it as a child. I began to suspect that 99 percent of my daily life was just as routinized and unnoticed; that my mind was always somewhere else; and that the thousand signals my body was sending me each minute were ignored. I guessed also that most people were like me in this respect.

Brushing my teeth attentively for two weeks, I gradually became aware of the tension in my elbow and fingers (was it there before?), the pressure of the brush on my gums, their slight bleeding (should I visit the dentist?). I looked up once and saw, really saw, my face in the mirror. I rarely looked at myself when I got up, perhaps because I wanted to avoid the puffy face I'd see, at least until it could be washed and smoothed to match the public image I prefer. (And how many times had I seen others do the same and believed I was different!)

This was an eye-opener to my privacy and to my humanity. An unremarkable picture of myself was beginning to surface, an image I'd created but never examined. It colored the images I made of the world and influenced how I dealt with my images of others. I saw this little by little.

But if this wider domain of resonance, spreading from the mere process of brushing my teeth, seems too far from its starting point, I should say immediately that it never left the bathroom. The physicality of brushing, the aromatic taste of toothpaste, rinsing my mouth and the brush, the many small nuances such as right-handedness causing me to enter my mouth with the loaded rush from that side and then move to the left side — these particularities always stayed in the present. The larger implications popped up from time to time during the subsequent days. All this from toothbrushing.[*]

---

[*] Alan Kaprow, "Art Which Can't Be Art (1986)," *Essays on the Blurring of Art and Life*, 219.

Meanwhile my father lost himself in the moment. In the photograph, for example, he sings on our brand-new karaoke machine as if no one were watching. But we are watching, all of us—not as spectators but actors, full of the wavering melody, the Christmas gifts, the warmth of the bubble lights on the tree.

In this way, my father's life was the height of Kaprow's ideals. Life forgot about art, which was the only way to find it.

In the photo, my father summons a low note out of his lungs. He is really singing. I am really playing with my trucks. Bob is pretending to be a wizard in his brand-new cloak, and my mother is filming, her hand raised to get our attention.

The action passed by too quickly to capture. The photos could never hold us.

Think of it this way: You never see my mother's face in the photographs. After my father met her, she took it upon herself to record everything. At first, when she wrote in the Rolodex, my father was angry at her for interfering. Then *he* stopped writing. It was my mother who gave the Rolodex to me.

My father thought he could stop the past from leaving him. My mother knew returning to it was the real art. Our family albums filled two wide shelves in our living room because she knew we would need them later. The photographs made new moments, even though the moments they captured were lost.

One day, however, my father took the photograph

above. My mom and I walk across a golf course, though neither of us remember where or when it was.

Why did he decide to preserve this image after so many years of living without documenting any-thing? What did he see in this long field, my mother and I walking through it as if unimaginably distant from him? I imagine Bob toddling at his side, clutching the corner of his pocket as he snapped the photograph.

He set the camera down, maybe for the last time. Then he picked up Bob and stared out at the grassy expanse until we turned and walked back toward him.

Finally, it was my last day in St. Louis. The garage was as clean as I could make it, aside from a pile of theater programs I intended to send to my brother and a box of items from the Happenings that I planned to take to Los Angeles. But there was one photograph that I still couldn't place.

I walked to the house, where my mother was making egg salad. I held the photo between my fingers, meaning to ask who it was. Instead I said, "Mom. Why did Dad stop with the Happenings?"

She stopped smashing eggs into the mayonnaise. She set her fork down.

"Was it because of us? Me?" I asked.

She shook her head.

"But it had to be. He had a family."

"It wasn't," she said. And it seemed for a moment that she knew more about the Happenings than I had believed. As if he'd never tried to shut her out of them, as if her contributions to the Rolodex were not exceptions but a rule. She said, "You weren't the reason he stopped writing them. You were the reason he started."

"What do you mean?"

"He wanted an event that didn't finish."

She looked at me patiently as I pretended to understand. Then I understood. She didn't believe in the distinction—life and art, art and life. Without his knowing, my mother had decided to be part of his Happening.

Now she had given me that choice. It was the last artifact of my father's life: the possibility that his Rolodex might never end.

I forgot to ask about the photograph that night, forgot again in the morning, and by now I don't think I ever will ask. The figure at the top of the ladder could be my mother just as easily as the figure crouching on the ground. But the forest does not look like Southern California, nor does it resemble our yard in St. Louis. It is

as if art exceeded life just this one time, our remainders
locked in emulsion.

The last photograph in the Rolodex is the Volkswagen. After I moved away from home, my mother sold it to another mother whose daughter was just learning to drive. Before they took the keys and pulled out of our driveway, my mother insisted on snapping a photo of the new owners with the convertible.

My father came home from the office to an empty driveway. He breathed a sigh of relief. The truth was, he had been asking my mother to get rid of the Cabriolet for years.

But *my* heart ached. I had learned to drive on the Cabriolet, turning up the tinny radio until the speakers shook in their casing. I had burned out the clutch in the hilly cemetery up the road. For the first time, I felt that strange sadness. I had never considered that living my life meant letting it go.

A week later, however, the woman who bought the car called to say the Cabriolet had broken down. She had changed her mind about buying it, she said. My mother, taken aback, said, "You can't change your mind." The woman began to shout. "I'm sorry," my mother said and hung up the phone. The woman called again and left a message, enraged.

My mother never called back, even though the woman called twice a week for a month. Those days were over, even if the days didn't know.

Though the Rolodex's last photograph is the Volkswagen, I added this and the following photo from my mother's archives. In a way, they are their own Happenings.

Still, I stand in the shade of my father, waiting. The Fourth of July Parade advances down Forest Park's wide byway. He drinks coffee that is almost down to the dregs. I lean forward as the firetruck nears. It blips its siren. Firemen hang from the side and wave. When I see my mom taking a photo of us, my eagerness swells into performance. Here I am in the crowd watching the event pass by. Here I am holding my pose for a second, and now my crimped flag and innocent excitement become part of the event in a way I never could have imagined. My dad, headless, is the frame. The parade rolls slowly toward us, and I am overcome by the thought of all I might feel once it arrives.

I still stand in front of my father, too, taking a photograph of us in our living room mirror. I wanted to preserve the act of preserving—as well as his hunched image, shirtless behind me, reading the paper on the couch. It is all here. Despite the years that separated him from the Happenings and the years that now separate me from the photo I took, we created more than we thought we created. We were lost in the event, gloriously submerged. It is only now, for the briefest moment, that we surface.

Acknowledgements

Thank you Keith Scribner for helping me make this book what it is and giving me advice about it that never stopped resonating. Thank you Jennifer Richter, Tara Williams, and Charlotte Headrick for your additional feedback about the book. Thank you Derek White for encouraging the book and, at an important moment, inspiring me to write the photographs section. Thank you Tim Jensen for assigning the reading that began the Rolodex.

Thank you to the editors of *New Delta Review*, *Sleepingfish*, and *Tammy*, where excerpts of this manuscript have previously appeared. Thank you to the many other editors who encouraged this book along the way.

Thank you to the team at Stillhouse Press, especially Rebecca Burke, Linda Hall, and Amanda Ganus. You showed me new pathways into the Rolodex and I am grateful to all of you.

Thank you Michelle Ross for selecting this book as the winner of the Stillhouse Press Novella Prize and for the words you shared about the book. Thank you Ashley Marie Farmer and Keith Scribner for your kind words about the book as well.

Thank you Mom and Dad for the photographs. You used the word "Happening" when I was little, and I remember wondering what it was. That question stayed with me. It gave this book life.

About the Author

Dennis James Sweeney is the author of *You're the Woods Too* (Essay Press, 2023) and *In the Antarctic Circle* (Autumn House Press, 2021). His writing has appeared in *Ecotone, Five Points, Ninth Letter, The New York Times,* and *The Southern Review,* among others. Formerly a Small Press Editor of *Entropy* and Assistant Editor of *Denver Quarterly,* he has an MFA from Oregon State University and a PhD from the University of Denver. Originally from Cincinnati, he lives in Amherst, Massachusetts, where he teaches at Amherst College.